For my dad

Henry Holt and Company, Publishers since 1866
Henry Holt® is a registered trademark of
Macmillan Publishing Group, LLC
120 Broadway, New York, NY 10271
mackids.com

Our books may be purchased in bulk for promotional, educational, or business use.
Please contact your local bookseller or the Macmillan Corporate and Premium Sales Department at
(800) 221-7945 ext. 5442 or by email at MacmillanSpecialMarkets@macmillan.com.

Library of Congress Control Number: 2021916955

First edition, 2022
Book design by Mike Burroughs
Printed in China by Hung Hing Off-set Printing Co. Ltd., Heshan City, Guangdong Province
The illustrations in this book were created using oil on gessoed paper.

ISBN 978-1-250-31737-7 (hardcover)
1 3 5 7 9 10 8 6 4 2

The WISHING BALLOONS

Jonathan D. Voss

Henry Holt and Company

New York

A new boy moved in to the neighborhood today.

"I'm Dot," I said. "What's your name?"

"Albert," he said back.

He looked sad.

I asked him if he wanted to play.

That night, I wondered if Albert was sad because he didn't want to move.

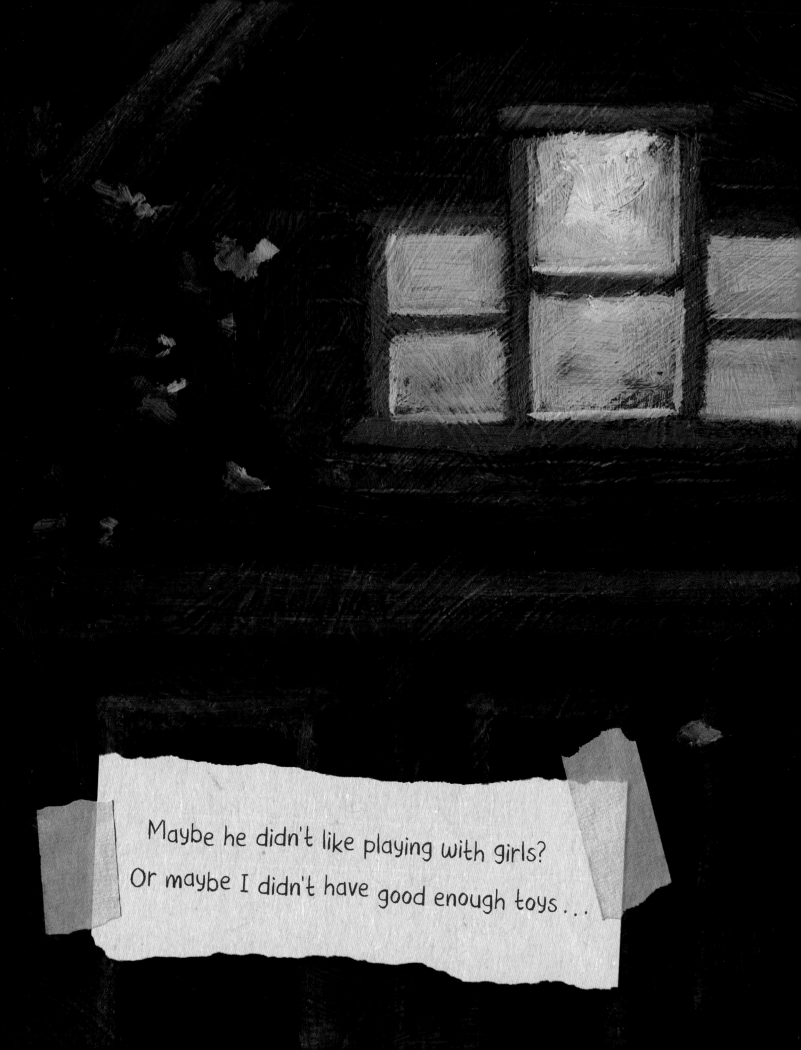

Just then, I heard a noise outside my window.

Tap.

Tap.

Tap.

It
was
a
balloon.

Tied to a note.

Dear Star

I only have one wish tonight. I wish I could fly far far away and maybe never have to come back.
Sincerely,
Albert

But it wasn't a note. It was a wish. I didn't know why it came to me. And I wasn't sure why he didn't want to stay.

I wondered if he wanted to go back to where he used to live. I thought about where I would go if I could fly. Then I remembered my kite . . .

It was a good thing my dad was there. Because if he wasn't, I might have flown away!

All of a sudden, I knew how to make Albert happy.

He smiled . . . just a little.

But he still did not want to play.

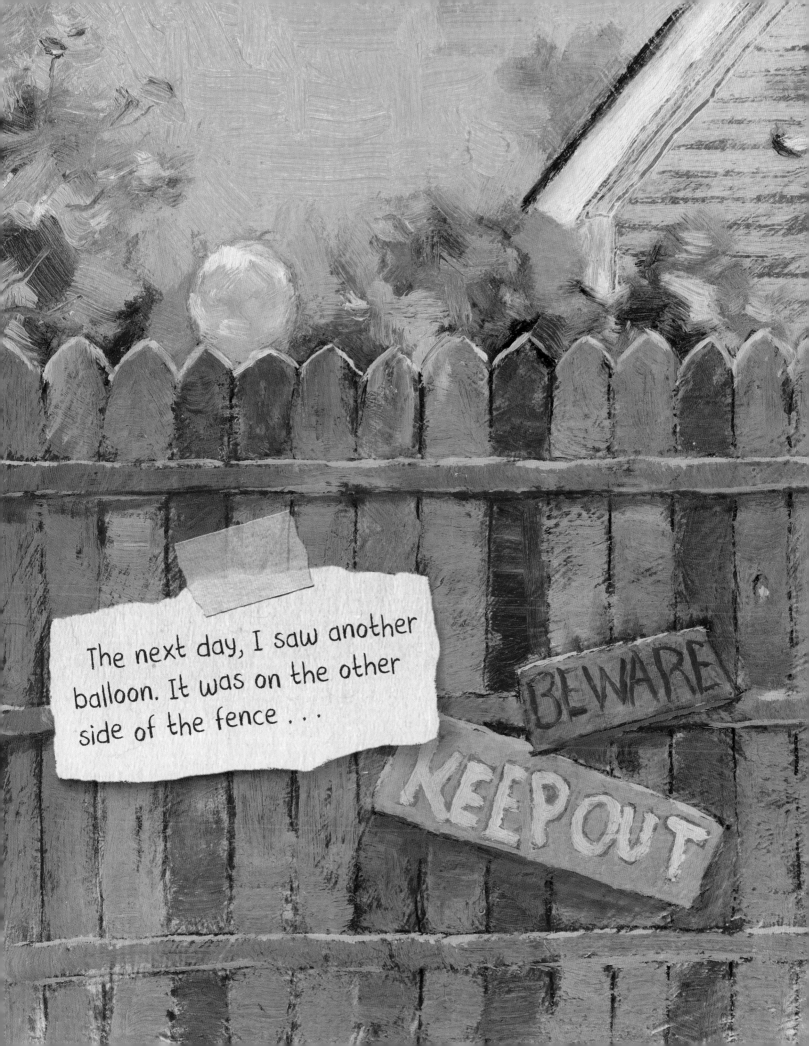

The next day, I saw another balloon. It was on the other side of the fence . . .

BEWARE!

KEEP OUT

Dear Star
I wish I had a dog. I
would like one that
is kind and gentle.
And if it's not too hard,
maybe he could be a
good listener too.
Sincerely,
Albert

I thought about Mrs. Finkleman—
her dog had puppies. But they had
already been given away.

I wondered if I could buy
a dog. But I was pretty
sure I wouldn't be allowed.
Besides, I only had two
dollars, a quarter, and five
pennies saved.
Then I thought about Bumby.

All of a sudden,

I knew for sure how to make Albert happy.

He smiled
again . . .

just
a little.

But he still did not want to play.

The next morning, I saw a
third balloon. It was at the
very top of Mr. Hsieh's tree.

I don't like to climb trees.
I don't like to go up high.
But I did it anyway.

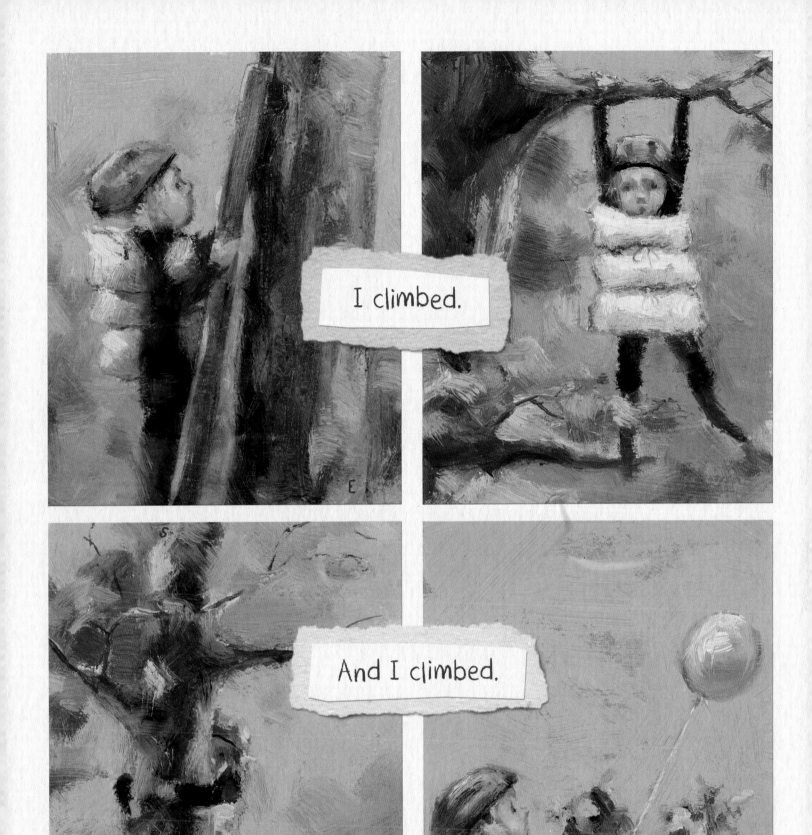

Dear Star

Tonight I have an extra big wish. It's about my dad. I miss him so much. I wish he was here again. I wish he could come back.

Sincerely,
Albert

I didn't know Albert's dad, or why he was gone. But I knew this wish was too hard for me to do.

I thought about Albert.

Then I thought about my dad.

And for a second, I thought: *What if he wasn't here anymore?*

All of a sudden . . . I knew.

Sometimes, it's okay to be sad. Sometimes, it's the only thing we can do.

I walked over to his house.

I didn't say a
single word.

And Albert, well . . .

. . . he stayed, too.